JimJim

and the Jelly Bean Journey

Written by Duane Ziegler

Illustrations by Vari Reichardt

Technicians Aaron Rogers

Julie Richards

Editor Alissa Hosman

DEDICATION

This book is dedicated to my wife Sandra for her love and support, my grandchildren for their inspiration, and my brother Jim and his family.

Jim and his family live near Sylvan Lake, high in the Rocky Mountains. Jim and his family are mice. They are very excited, because they are traveling to the other side of the lake. They have packed bags of food and notebook paper. Everyone is happy, because Father Mouse has just honored Jim with his new name of JimJim.

Joe, JimJim's brother, asks, "How do you like your new name?"

"Biff, bang, bang, bang. I'm so happy, happy, happy", JimJim responds.

Father Mouse then says, "We are letting you go out into the woods all alone. We wish that you have fun and have a safe return home."

"Look out for each other", Mother Mouse adds. They hug their parents and promise to be careful.

They start in bright sunshine along the west side of the lake, going north. JimJim takes the lead, followed by Mary, Katie, and Joe. After walking a little, JimJim checks on everyone.

JimJim speaks to Joe, "What things must we always watch for?"

"We must always watch for dark rain clouds and fast-moving shadows that could mean an attacking bird, like a hawk", Joe responds. Soon, they hear sounds near the water. Someone is singing: "Chugalug, chugalug, I'm Mr. Stinkbug. Chugalug, chugalug, I'm Mr. Stinkbug. My name is Mr. Stinkbug. Chugalug, chugalug. My name is Mr. Stinkbug, chugalug, chugalug."

Mary, the littlest sister, laughs the loudest and pleads, "We are close enough, don't get any closer."

Katie, JimJim's other sister, draws a picture of Mr. Stinkbug

Joe and Mary get very close to Mr. Stinkbug and Joe quietly whispers something to him. Mr. Stinkbug answers, "You should do it right away, because it wasn't long ago that I saw Rusty, the Hawk, flying this way."

Joe spends a couple minutes with Mr. Stinkbug and then runs to the edge of the lake and puts something on the ground.

Mr. Stinkbug hollers: "Shadows again."

Joe screams loudly so everybody can hear, "Low shadows. Low shadows. It is Rusty the Hawk! Danger! Everybody hide!

Everyone scurries *to* find a hiding place. Soon they hear the wings of Rusty the Hawk. Rusty is right above them. He dives and snatches something along the edge of the lake.

JimJim shouts, "Oh no! It looks like Rusty has grabbed Joe, because that definitely is Joe's green jacket and Rusty is squeezing his claws."

JimJim runs out from his hiding spot and into the open, shouting: "Joe, why were you talking with Mr. Stinkbug? What were you thinking? Now you're gone. Why? Why?"

Suddenly, there are loud screams from high above the lake. Rusty screeches: "Yucky, Yucky, Stinky, Stinky, No, No, No!" An object falls from the sky and lands in the lake.

Joe comes out of hiding and starts to cheer, "We did it. We did it. We tricked Rusty. Mr. Stinkbug and I made a dummy mouse by rolling up my green jacket and tying it up. We smeared lots of stinky stuff off of Mr. Stinkbug's back. With Rusty's crying, he must smell pretty bad. Poor, poor Rusty. Let's thank Mr. Stinkbug. He is our hero! Hurray, hurray. Everyone line up and thank Mr. Stinkbug."

Mary barely touches the shiny black shell with one finger; Katie touches with two fingers and Joe does a fist bump; JimJim does a high five with Mr. Stinkbug.

Mr. Stinkbug declares, "This is the best day of my life! I have friends."

JimJim hugs his brother, smiles and tells him, "I am proud of you. Well done. We better keep going and keep our eyes and ears open. You never know what might happen next."

JimJim leads the family down the trail again. They go around a big tree and find an old mouse with a gray beard. JimJim introduces himself, "Hello, my name is JimJim and this is Joe, Mary, and Katie."

The old mouse has a certain gleam in his eyes and reveals, "I am known as Old Man Mouse. Will you join me for a snack?"

Old Man Mouse had been eating something out of an opened bag. He smiles and starts singing, "Jellybeans in my tummy. Yummy, yummy in my tummy. Yummy, yummy in my tummy, tummy, tummy" as he shares with each young mouse a handful out of his stash of delicious jellybeans.

Old Man Mouse has a neatly trimmed beard, and is wearing brown trousers. His shirt is light tan with a musical note design. Also, Old Man Mouse has special shoes. His shoes are polished black with a silver buckle on top. On each buckle, the letter Z is imprinted.

Joe, like everyone else, is fascinated by Old Man Mouse and inquires, "May we ask what the letter Z stands for?"

Old Man Mouse answers, "When I was younger, there was Billy Bully, the Rat. He was a mean guy. One day he stole my candy, so I used a little karate and went chop, chop, chop and Billy went chuck, chuck, chuck, and threw up all over his shoes. My father was so happy, he named me ZanderZander."

Katie and Mary say "amazing" at the same time and Katie gets out a piece of paper to draw Old Man Mouse. Everyone is interested in visiting with him.

Just then, there is a bright, startling flash of lightning. Then there are loud booms of thunder. The lightning is so bright, that JimJim and Joe try to cover their eyes to hide them from the flash.

It's a downpour. JimJim and Joe see that Old Man Mouse is holding his arms around their sisters.

Old Man Mouse hollers, "Let's go to the cave just up ahead." Then another crack of lightning blinds the boys, forcing them to run for cover into the trees. JimJim and Joe make their way deeper into the trees, searching for a safe place. Finally, they find a hollow aspen log and climb into it to keep dry.

JimJim whispers, "I sure hope Katie and Mary, are safe. I'm very worried."

The next morning, they agree that they are indeed, totally lost. Joe mutters, "How are we ever going to find Katie and Mary? I'm sure glad Old Man Mouse is with them."

Nothing looks familiar. JimJim and Joe sit down and each snack on a brightly colored jellybean.

Just then, they hear a tapping sound. They look up towards the noise and see a woodpecker chipping on a branch high in the tree above them. As the bird spots them, he has a welcome message: "Good morning, I am Tony, the Woodpecker. I am a Downy Woodpecker. I have black wings, white back and belly, black bars on my tail feathers, white markings on my wings, and a red patch on the top of my head. My job is tapping on branches to find insect tunnels. I find my food and am happy all day long."

Tony the Woodpecker questions the mice, "Are you strangers? I have not seen you before." "We are lost and have no ideas about finding our way home", JimJim complains.

Tony tells them, "I know of a way." Tony starts chipping out holes on a tree branch. Soon Tony has drilled four holes into the tree branch. Tony states, "Because insects had already drilled out tunnels, the branch is hollow. Sound can be created by covering one of the holes and blowing on the ends of the stick."

He demonstrates by covering one hole and playing a wonderful note and the boys' eyes fill with wonder. Tony then blocks another hole and blows again, making a different sound. After playing the second note he holds the instrument up.

Tony explains, "This is called a flute, and the sounds coming out of it are called music notes."

The mice can't wait to try it out for themselves. So, with Tony's help, Joe dances over the holes as JimJim blows on the end of the flute. Musical sounds soon weave themselves into a song.

Tony encourages, "When some other animals, or birds, come to see what the noise is all about, they will find you!"

With that good news, JimJim and Joe continue smiling, and blowing, and dancing.

They love making the flute music! As Tony had said, curious animals and birds start gathering around, coming closer and closer. One of those visitors is Alissa, a dove. Alissa asks, "Are you JimJim and Joe? There is a search party looking for you."

JimJim asks eagerly, "Have you seen Katie and Mary? Are they safe?"

"Yes, they are fine. I will lead you to them", Alissa says.

JimJim turns to Tony and says, "Thank you for helping us and we will always treasure the flute you helped us make." Tony smiles, and waves goodbye.

Meanwhile, in the cave, Old Man Mouse has been trying to keep Katie and Mary somewhat calm. Mary has been crying herself to sleep, and not eating much. Katie has been holding Mary in her arms, and also breaking down and crying. Mary has been repeating, "How are we ever going to find JimJim and Joe?"

Old Man Mouse, with a comforting tone answers, "We have many friends of the forest. Someone will help us."

Finally, a swarm of fireflies sweeps down by the cave and Old Man Mouse inquires, "Anyone know Princess Twinkle Toes, the Forest Princess; or Princess Orahava, Princess of Love?"

It wasn't very long before the fireflies arrived with Princess Orahava.

Old Man Mouse speaks, "Thank you for coming. I have two friends that were stranded by the storm. They have two lost brothers. Could you perform a search for them? Their names are JimJim and Joe."

Princess Orahava smiles, and replies "I will gladly do that for you. What are the names of your small friends here?"

Old Man Mouse whispers, "They are Katie and Mary. Could you bring some of your friends by to visit them? They are lonely."

Katie and Mary feel a little more comfortable now and start nibbling on sweet jellybeans. Later, the little mice fall asleep. In the morning there is singing outside the cave.

Katie and Mary run to the cave entrance. Katie asks, "Who are you?"

The birds chirp, "We are the school of singing birds and we love singing, Yadda, yadda, yeah, yeah, yippee, yippee, yo, yo, yupper, yupper. Yesterday your yellow yogurt yelled yahoo. Ha, ha, he, he, ho, ho, hey, hey. Happy Henry has his home here. La, la, lo, lo, lily, lily, lollipop, lollipop. Lucy, lucy, lucky, lucky, licky, licky."

Smiling, the birds wave goodbye and fly away.

Katie sits down to draw a picture of them.

Mary asks the next visitor, "Who are you?" The next arrival is a bright yellow caterpillar and she informs everyone, "Hi, I'm Dilly Dally Sally. I'm pleased to meet you. I know your very next visitors are very quiet. They are the two Worm Brothers. Their names are Iggily-Piggily and Wiggily-Swiggily. Their wives, Giggily-Tiggily and Jiggily-Figgily, are holding up their babies, Ciggily-Higgily and Biggily-Miggily."

They all smile for their picture being drawn by Katie, and slowly go on their way.

Katie asks some baby ducks, "What are you doing?"

The ducklings answer, "We are practicing wing exercises." They pump their wings and shout: "One, one; two, two; three, three; four, four. We love to sing: We walk like a duck, we squawk like a duck, we waddle like a duck, we are proud to be a duck." One little duck waddles forward and says, "Please come visit us, my name is Donald."

They wave and smile as they leave the cave entrance.

When Mrs. Skunk and her three little babies come to visit, Mary exclaims, "How cute you are!"

BAM BAM BAM comes a loud noise from back of the cave. Mr. Black Bear is waking up and he's letting everybody know he is mad. It seems like everyone runs screaming away from the cave.

But not everyone goes running. Mrs. Skunk and her babies stay at the cave. Mrs. Skunk snaps to Mr. Black Bear, "You spoiled our visit with the mice."

Mr. Black Bear growls, "I don't care about anything you say or do."

Mrs. Skunk retorts, "You are not nice, so we will share our perfume with you." She and her babies line up and spray and spray and spray Mr. Black Bear. He howls and cries and runs out of the cave into the woods like a baby.

Just then, up in the air, many voices are heard. Old Man Mouse whispers a favor to his friends, and when JimJim and Joe arrive to be reunited with their sisters, The Cricket Band is playing music, everybody is dancing, and singing, and sharing food, especially jellybeans.

JimJim sits down next to Old Man Mouse and says, "I'd like to thank you so much for taking care of Katie and Mary. We were very worried. We want you to meet our parents. You are a very special friend, with the unusual name of ZanderZander."

Old Man Mouse smiles and replies, "You have a fine family and I would love to meet your parents. You have the unusual name of JimJim. Would you tell me about the experience that led to you earning your name?"

JimJim answers, "Father was impressed by my outsmarting Mr. Owl. One day I'm walking on the trail. I go around a corner and there's Mr. Owl, standing about five feet away, though it looks like he's right on top of me."

'Mr. Owl hoots, 'I have you just where I want you.' and I look at Mr. Owl and state: 'I am Jim. I'm defabulated. I was fabulous, but, now I'm just blub, blub, blub.'

'Mr. Owl mutters and stutters, 'What? What is defabulated?' Mr. Owl turns his head one way and then the other. He then rolls up his eyes up high and shakes his head again. When he looks down, I am gone. I had run off into the bushes. Mr. Owl is hollering and gibbering, 'Hey, where did you go?'

Other birds hear Mr. Owl hollering and they spread the news that I had outsmarted Mr. Owl. I am now known as a fabulous mouse, and as JimJim."

Old Man Mouse nods his head, smiles and says, "JimJim, you are definitely fabulous."

All of a sudden, Joe shouts, "Attention everyone, the wind is blowing harder and harder. Another storm is coming. We need to find shelter."

Finally, after searching and searching, the mice find a nice place under tree roots.

That night, JimJim and his family are exhausted. But, during the night, they all wake up, because they hear Mr. Owl making sounds that seem dangerously close to them. Mr. Owl is hooting, "Whoo. Whoo. I'm hunting you. You tricked me, now I want revenge."

The mice hear Mr. Owl's wings whip as he lands on the tree they are hiding under. All of the mice move further back under the tree roots.

Ker-plop! Mr. Owl lands on the ground next to the tree.

Silence. Not one mouse moves. Finally, they hear the wings of Mr. Owl, as he flies away. JimJim heaves a big sigh of relief and thinks to himself, "Silence never sounded so good. We are safe."

Suddenly, a wet soft area under the tree roots gives way. Mary cries out, "Help me! I am falling into a hole!" She shouts up from down below, "I am scared. I think I am okay, but I can't climb up."

JimJim, trying to remain calm, comforts, "Mary, are you hurt? Is it too steep to climb out of the hole?"

Joe, looking down the hole, inquires, "Mary, if we push dirt down the hole, could you climb up?"

Mary, crying loudly now, mumbles, "Yes, I could try."

JimJim, Joe, and Katie, each take turns pushing dirt down the hole, trying not to bury their littlest sister. Finally, Mary shouts, "Stop. Let me try to get out." Mary slowly inches her way up, taking big steps, and finally climbs out of the hole. Everyone hugs her! JimJim, Joe, Mary, and Katie did not sleep any more that night.

That morning, after a breakfast snack, Katie and Mary practice saying a certain sentence softer, then louder, and louder. Together they recite, "We have had fun, scary adventures, made new friends; but we want to go home."

JimJim smiles and responds, "Well, we need to find some berries and flowers for our parents and surprise them!"

Everyone began the search, but they stop to see a beautiful butterfly, dancing in front of them. The butterfly remarks, "Hi, I am Dilly Dally Sally. I was once a caterpillar and now I have changed. Do you remember me? I was the yellow caterpillar. Everyone changes. We change shapes and forms. We become bigger, older every day. The most important thing is always smile and be happy. Please follow me; I know exactly where you can find some pretty flowers and berries."

Katie doodles up one last picture to take home to Mother and Father. The mice pick berries and flowers and start running home.

Everyone hugs and kisses and tells Mother and Father about all their adventures.

Father Mouse stands up and announces, "Well, it sure looks like our children are all grown up now. So that means, from now on, our children will be named JimJim, JoeJoe, KatieKatie, and MaryMary. We are very proud of all of you. How do you like your new names?"

JoeJoe booms, "Bazinga! Bazinga! Bazinga!"

"Wow! Pow! Pow! Pow!" declares KatieKatie.

MaryMary loudly shouts, "Say Hey! Hey! Hey!"

"What did you learn?" Mother asks. MaryMary thinks for a moment and answers, "Wow. I learned that a caterpillar changes into a butterfly. I learned how much my family loves me, and how much I love them."
KatieKatie says, "We have many friends in the forest. I learned that there are dangers everywhere, and we must always be prepared. I drew some pictures along the way." KatieKatie pulls her drawings out of her bag to share with everyone.

JoeJoe grins. "I really learned how to respect others. I listened to Mr. Stinkbug and he warned us about Rusty the Hawk. Now, he's our good friend."

JimJim says, "We learned that you can't let the bad things ruin your day because they aren't really bad, they're just lessons. We also learned that when you give kindness, you get kindness in return. Thank you for giving us this opportunity to go out by ourselves."

JimJim reaches into his pocket and adds, "Here are some jellybeans from our new friend, Old Man Mouse."

Father Mouse and Mother Mouse share a red jellybean then, shout, "Fire Cracker! Hot! Hot! Hot!" They had never tasted cinnamon before.

Father Mouse says, "It is time for a family hug." The mouse family forms a circle for a big hug with everyone laughing.

~The End~

ABOUT THE AUTHOR

Duane Ziegler was raised on a farm in North Dakota with five brothers. The attraction of wheat fields, pasture land, and rolling prairies was strong. But, the mountains of Colorado have been the biggest influence in his life. Duane Ziegler has been a professional educator for twenty years and a professional real estate agent for twenty-three years. He is a member of SCBWI, Colorado Authors League, and Roaring Fork Writer's Group. His immediate family includes his wife, Sandy, two children, DeAnn and Nathan and three grandchildren. He thanks the many people supporting him in creating children's fiction.

ABOUT THE ILLUSTRATOR

Vari Reichardt grew up on a cattle ranch in the Colorado Mountains. Art was a large part of her life as she spent her time outside taking care of the animals and hiking in the hills. She went on to get a Bachelor's Degree of Art, with published art work in the Historical Journal of Western Colorado. Vari has taught art to children for years and is also a full-time pre-school teacher. She is married and has seven children that she homeschools in the same town where she grew up.

Made in the USA
San Bernardino, CA
22 March 2017